For all my little friends with big, big feelings,
you are always lovable, you are always loved,
and you can do hard things.
—A.P.

For kids with big feelings and tremendous hearts
but especially for S., who showed me the way.
—S.K.

Alexandra Penfold  Suzanne Kaufman

BIG
Feelings

Alfred A. Knopf   New York

It's time to play.

Big plans today!

But sometimes things
get in the way . . .

Feeling bold.

Feeling mad.

Goodbye, happy.

Hello, sad.

I have big feelings.

You have them, too.

How can I help?
What can we do?

Talk it out?
Talk it through?

I am sorry.
I am, too!

New plans today,
and that's okay.

We won't let this get in the way.

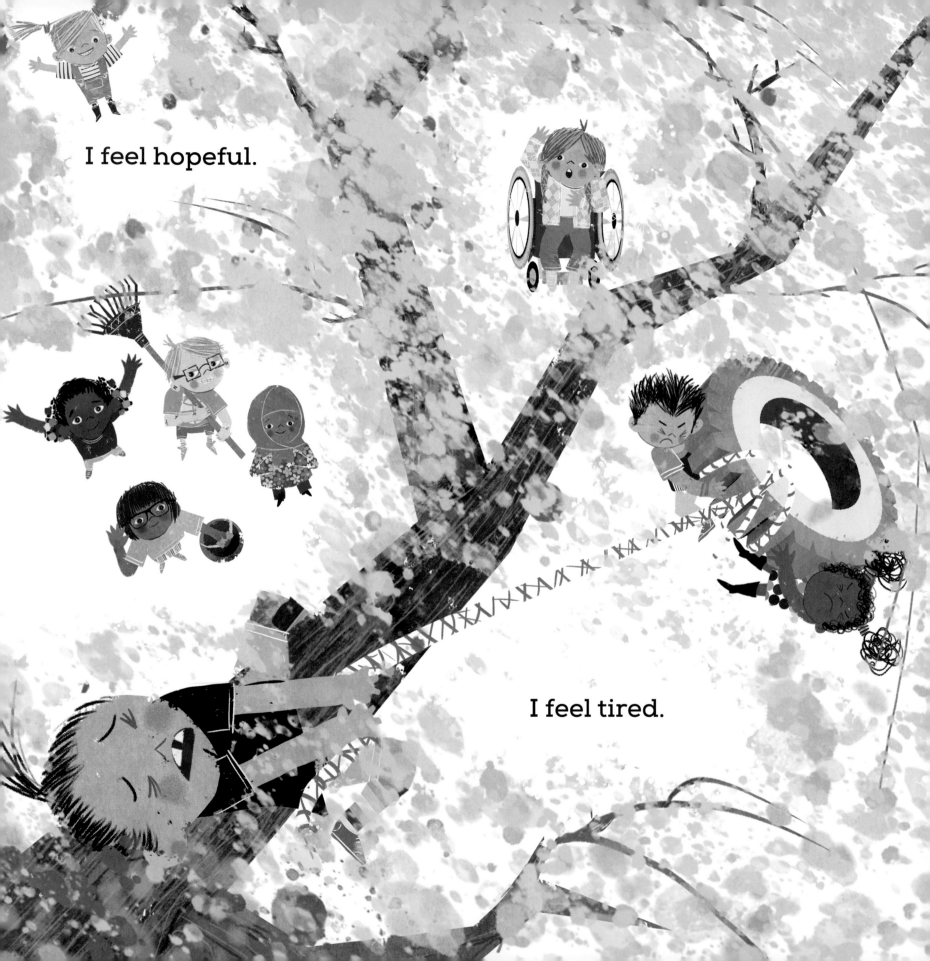

I feel hopeful.

I feel tired.

I feel frustrated.

I feel . . . *inspired.*

I have big feelings.
You have them, too.

How can I help?
What can we do?

I feel frustrated.

I feel . . . *inspired.*

I have big feelings.
You have them, too.

How can I help?
What can we do?

Work together.
Build a crew.

Begin again.
Start anew.

I feel excited.

I feel scared.

I feel nervous.

I feel prepared!

I feel hopeless.
I feel low.

I want to quit.
Give up and go.

We all have big feelings,
both me and you.

How can we help?
What can we do?

See another point of view?

This is our world.
This is our home.

Whatever we're feeling,
we're never alone.

THIS IS A BORZOI BOOK PUBLISHED BY ALFRED A. KNOPF

Text copyright © 2021 by Alexandra Penfold
Jacket art and interior illustrations copyright © 2021 by Suzanne Kaufman

All rights reserved. Published in the United States by Alfred A. Knopf,
an imprint of Random House Children's Books,
a division of Penguin Random House LLC, New York.

Knopf, Borzoi Books, and the colophon are registered trademarks
of Penguin Random House LLC.

Visit us on the Web! rhcbooks.com

Educators and librarians, for a variety of teaching tools, visit us at RHTeachersLibrarians.com

Library of Congress Cataloging-in-Publication Data
Names: Penfold, Alexandra, author. | Kaufman, Suzanne, illustrator.
Title: Big feelings / Alexandra Penfold, Suzanne Kaufman.
Description: First edition. | New York: Alfred A. Knopf, 2021. |
Audience: Ages 4–8. | Audience: Grades 2–3. |
Summary: "A group of kids express a multitude of feelings and discover they are not alone." —Provided by publisher
Identifiers: LCCN 2019056161 (print) | LCCN 2019056162 (ebook) | ISBN 978-0-525-57974-8 (hardcover) |
ISBN 978-0-525-57975-5 (library binding) | ISBN 978-0-525-57976-2 (ebook)
Subjects: CYAC: Stories in rhyme. | Emotions—Fiction.
Classification: LCC PZ8.3.P376 Big 2021 (print) | LCC PZ8.3.P376 (ebook) DDC [E]—dc23

The text of this book is set in 19-point Nexa Slab Bold.
The illustrations were created using acrylic paint, ink, crayon, and collage with Adobe Photoshop.
Book design by Martha Rago

MANUFACTURED IN CHINA
March 2021
10 9 8 7 6 5 4 3 2 1
First Edition

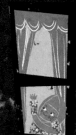